The
Golden Bird

First published in Great Britain 1995 by Heinemann Young Books
an imprint of Reed International Books Limited.
Michelin House, 81 Fulham Rd, London SW3 6RB
Mammoth paperback edition first published 1998
Published in hardback by Heinemann Educational Publishers,
a division of Reed Educational and Professional Publishing Limited
by arrangement with Reed International Books Limited.
Text copyright © Berlie Doherty 1995
Illustrations copyright © John Lawrence 1995
Additional illustrations copyright © John Lawrence 1998

The Author and Illustrator have asserted their moral rights

Paperback ISBN 0 7497 3380 2
Hardback ISBN 0 434 80298 0
10 9 8 7 6 5 4 3 2 1
A CIP catalogue record for this title is available from the British Library
Printed at Oriental Press Limited, Dubai

Berlie Doherty

The *Golden Bird*

Illustrated by JOHN LAWRENCE

YELLOW BANANAS

For Andrew, Rob and Peter
– and all the New Vic Crew

Chapter One

'BY THE WAY,' said Mr Swain as his class was clearing up at the end of the afternoon. 'I've finished writing the school play.'

He had everyone's immediate attention. Only Andrew kept his head down.

'It's based on the story of the Sleeping Beauty,' Mr Swain went on.

Lynne beamed round at everyone then closed her eyes.

'And I've cast it,' said Mr Swain. 'Eddie is to be the king.'

Eddie heaved a sigh of relief and grinned at

Craig. He waved his hand in a lordly fashion.
He would be regal and mighty. He would
shout out his lines and make his courtiers
quiver. The audience would quiver. Everyone
would be afraid of him.

Craig sniffed. He was bored already. He
wanted to be out in the playground, kicking

his football around.

'Sarah is queen.' Sarah blushed and put her hands over her face. Under their cover she

smiled to herself. She would wear a sparkly crown and flashing jewellery, and a wonderful flowing silver dress. Everybody would say how beautiful she was. Lynne opened her eyes and poked her.

'Richard is the cook.'

'Cook!' Richard was alarmed. 'That's a girl's part.'

'Shows how much you know,' said Lynne. 'All the cooks in the posh hotels are men. They wear floppy hats and . . .'

'And strings of sausages round their necks,' said Mr Swain. 'You'll be a very good cook, Richard. It's an important character part. Nearly the main part.'

'Who's Sleeping Beauty?' Lynne demanded. 'That's the main part.'

'Georgina,' said Mr. Swain.

Georgina stared at him.

'Georgina!' shouted Lynne. 'GeorgINA?'

'She's only been here a week,' grumbled Shaz.

'And she's not exactly beautiful, either,' said Lynne. 'Not what I call beautiful.'

'Georgina has a lovely singing voice,' said Mr Swain. 'And that's one of the reasons why I've given her the part.'

If Georgina had had the courage, she would have run up to the front of the classroom and given Mr Swain a hug. Yesterday at break-time he had talked to her and she had told him that one day she wanted to be a famous singer and then he had asked her to sing her favourite song to him. She had been so nervous then that her voice had come out in little broken trickles, full of fog and tremble, but he hadn't seemed to notice.

'And the prince is Craig.'

Scarlet-faced, Craig put his head down and his hands over his ears.

'You have to kiss her! You have to kiss Georgina!' Eddie crowed. 'I wouldn't be the prince for ANYthing!'

Everyone laughed, even Lynne. 'I'm glad I'm not Sleeping Beauty,' she said. 'Craig's always dribbling. Fancy being kissed by CRAIG! Yuk!'

'The fairies are . . .'

The teacher's voice was drowned in laughter as the boys turned round and jeered at the girls.

'QUIET! The fairies are Peter, Tim, Howard, Steve, Chad, Rob . . .'

At the back of the classroom Andrew sat and stared out of the window. He let the laughter and jeers wash over him. It was always like this, since the day he had stopped being happy. He couldn't talk properly any more. He went to a special teacher once a week and even she was in despair over him.

He stammered and stuttered, his teeth stuck together and his jaw jammed shut. And everyone laughed at him.

It was easier if he didn't talk at all. At least when he didn't talk people stopped noticing him. If they didn't notice him they didn't laugh at him. He liked it better that way. He pretended he was a ghost, and that nobody knew he was there. He just wished the afternoon bell would go and he could get away and go home.

'But the fairies are BOYS!' spluttered Lynne. 'That's stupid!'

'Except for the wicked fairy,' smiled Mr Swain. 'And that's you.'

Chapter Two

AT LAST THE bell went. The class rushed out in a flurry of laughing and joking. Everyone was excited at the thought of the school play, even though Mr Swain had some odd ideas about casting. That was because he was new, they decided. Mr Swain gave them all notes to their parents explaining that they would have to stay behind after school some evenings for rehearsals.

As always, Andrew waited until all the others had left before he stood up. Mr Swain was busy marking at the desk, and Andrew tiptoed up the aisle, careful not to touch any of the desks or chairs as he passed them, in case he made a noise. He had almost reached the door when Mr Swain looked up from his work.

'By the way, Andrew,' he said. 'I've written in a part for you.'

Andrew stopped. He didn't look at the teacher, but kept his eyes fixed on the door handle. As soon as Mr Swain finished speaking he would slip out into the yard.

'I'd like you to play the part of the golden bird.' Mr Swain looked up. 'If you'd like to, that is.'

Andrew said nothing.

'Think about it, Andrew.'

Rehearsals began the next day. Mr Swain brought copies of the script for everyone to look at.

'The play begins with a song,' he said. 'And I want everyone to sing it together. Have a go now, just saying the words.'

Slowly the class began, all reciting in a higgledy piggledy fashion, so  the words bumped into each other. But Andrew just stared out of the window.

Birds were playing in the field, lifting themselves up and away, swooping and gliding, soaring up towards the clouds.

'Start again,' said Mr Swain.

*We will tell you a story
Of once upon a time,
Of a king and a queen who
were granted a wish,
Of a princess who slept for a
hundred years,
And a prince who woke her
up with a kiss;
Of a wicked fairy's evil curse,
And a golden bird with
magic power . . .'*

'Hang on!' Lynne interrupted the chanting.
'You didn't tell us about the golden bird.
Who's she?'

Mr Swain looked round the classroom at
no one in particular.

'Do we have a golden bird?' he asked.

Andrew made himself turn away from the
window. He didn't dare trust himself to
speak. All he knew, with every bone in his
body, was that he wanted to be the golden
bird. He nodded his head very slightly and
then looked away again.

'Yes, we do have a golden bird,' said Mr
Swain. 'And I'll tell you all later who it is.

Now. You did that chant quite well, in the end. Mr Palmer will be writing some music for it. First you'll all come on as jugglers and musicians – a really lively start to the play before it quietens into a magic story. Can anyone here juggle?'

Shaz put up her hand, 'My mum's learning circus skills at night-school. I can juggle, walk on stilts, spin plates, eat fire . . .'

'Juggling will do, Shaz. Pick two boys and two girls and you can teach them to juggle with these special juggling balls. NOTHING ELSE IS TO BE USED. I don't want anybody getting knocked out before the play evens starts.

The rest of you choose instruments. All the fairies can have bells round their ankles.'

Lynne pushed Tim and Howard over in her eagerness to get to the bells first.

'Except Lynne,' Mr Swain said.

She stood with her mouth wide open, staring at him in disbelief. 'That's not fair. That's just not fair!'

'I don't think it would do for the wicked fairy to have bells round her ankles. Just be satisfied with having the most exciting part in the play. Go away somewhere and practise a really wicked cackle, will you?'

Weeping, Lynne retreated to the end of the hall, snatching one of the juggling balls in mid-air as she passed.

Mr Swain gazed around him. It was bedlam. Yellow, red and green juggling balls were cascading round the room. The jugglers were shouting and laughing at each other, squirming under their chairs and through legs.

Minstrels were shaking bells and banging
drums and tambourines. A recorder group
was practising scales. Lynne was laughing
loudly and wickedly. The head-teacher peered
round the door, waved, and backed out
quickly.

Andrew was standing with his back to
everyone. His chin rested on his hands, his
elbows on the window ledge.

He stared and stared at the movements of
the birds in the yard outside.

He didn't move again until everyone had gone home. Mr Swain had gone off to the music cupboard to lock away all the instruments. Andrew turned away from the window. The birds had all flown away from the shouting children, but he didn't need to watch them any more.

He started with his neck. He hunched his shoulders slightly so his head jutted forward. Now he practised moving his head. He jerked it from side to side in quick, light movements. He pretended his nose was a beak. He lifted his head and peered down his nose, pretending he could only see a tiny area each side of it. He cocked his head from side to side to look in other directions, always being careful to look straight down his beak.

Now he would concentrate on his wings. He stood up as straight as he could, with his shoulders still slightly hunched and his head to one side. His wings would sprout from his shoulder blades. He shrugged his shoulders to loosen them up and then spread out the feathers of his fingers. He flexed his shoulder muscles and gently rippled his arms up and down, like waves. His movements became slower and steadier and stronger. Then he lifted his head, opened his beak, and pretended to sing.

Chapter Three

THERE WAS A roar of excitement from the
class on the day that Mr Swain and Miss Evans
brought in the costumes. Some of them hung
loosely from coat hangers and others were
piled up in a big wicker basket. All the
children had to sit down and wait with their
arms folded until they were called to have
their costumes handed out to them.

'The fairies first,' smiled Miss Evans.

The six boy fairies all groaned, and their
friends jeered and whistled. Lynne had told

them that they would be wearing white ballet dresses with tinselly wings, and holding sticks with silver stars on them for wands. One by one Miss Evans drew from her basket six wonderful sky coloured cloaks with deep hoods. They had rivers and mountains and leaves and flowers sewn into them, and when the boys put them on, they flowed round them with every movement they made.

'Wonderful,' said Mr Swain. 'You really do look like magic people.'

'What about their wings?' Lynne demanded.

'No wings,' said Miss Evans. 'We've decided there's only going to be one character with wings, and that will be the golden bird.'

'Who is the golden bird?' Craig asked. Everyone looked round. Andrew stared in front of him.

'I think Mr Swain is going

to do it!' Shaz giggled..

'The wicked fairy's costume is the same, but black,' said Miss Evans.

Lynne was upset.

She had been practising ballet steps all week at home. She couldn't possibly do ballet steps in that long cloak without falling over it. Mr Swain draped the cloak round her and she practised swirling across the room.

'Hiss!' everyone hissed.

She cackled hideously.

Miss Evans handed out the rest of the costumes and the children were allowed to walk round for a bit to get used to them before the rehearsal started. The fairies swept round the room, with their cloaks flowing. Eddie and Sarah tried to swirl their royal cloaks and tripped over the hems. The recorder players squeaked into giggles.

'Mine's too long!' Sarah moaned. 'Everybody's laughing at me.'

'And my crown's too big!' said Eddie. 'I
can't possibly frighten everybody with my
crown slipping over my nose like this.'

'You'll make a wonderful comedy act!' Mr
Swain laughed. 'I'm fed up of seeing stuffy
kings and queens in plays. You'll cheer
everyone up, the pair of you.'

Sarah flounced away in disgust and tripped
over her cloak again. She looked round
anxiously.

In the midst of all the excitement Miss Evans came over to Andrew and asked him to follow her to her room.

'I haven't decided what kind of costume to make for you, Andrew,' she said. 'I wondered about just giving you a puppet of a golden bird to hold. It might be the easiest.'

Andrew looked alarmed. He wouldn't be able to move his wings if he was holding a puppet.

'Or I could make you a gold costume and fasten some stiff wings to the back. 'They're rather heavy so you'd have to stand very still, but you wouldn't mind that, would you?'

He bowed his head, and Miss Evans sighed. She might as well be talking to herself.

'You only have to stand behind the Sleeping Beauty while everyone sings your golden bird song, don't you? It's not as if you're expected to do anything, Andrew. We just want you to look good.'

Andrew waited until he was quite sure that Miss Evans didn't have anything else to say to him. Then when she was looking through her pile of materials, he slipped out of her room. She looked up, holding some wire that she thought of twisting into a beak for him, and sighed again.

After the rehearsal had finished, Mr Swain packed away all the costumes in the wicker basket and wheeled them back to Miss Evans' room. He realised he had forgotten the cook's floppy hat and went back you fetch it. Andrew was alone in the hall. He was standing with his back to him. He didn't hear Mr Swain come in. Mr Swain backed out again silently and hurried down to Miss Evans' room.

'Come quickly,' he said. 'I think we've
solved the problem of the golden bird's
costume.'

They crept to the doorway of the hall and
peeped in, hardly daring to breathe in case
Andrew saw them. There he was, moving
slowly and gracefully up and down the hall.
His head was cocked to one side,
his eyes were bright and shining, and
his wings were rippling for flight.

Chapter Four

AT LAST THE day of the performance came. It was to be held in the evening, and the day seemed to last for ever. The only thing the children wanted to think about was the play. They argued about who had the most people coming to see it.

'I've got the most,' said Shaz. 'My mum's bringing all her circus class friends – so you'd better be good!' she warned the jugglers.

'All my aunties are coming,' said Lynne.

'And I've got nine!'

Andrew was the only one who didn't join in the general chatter. He hadn't even mentioned the play to his mother. He hardly talked, even at home, since the day he had started to be unhappy. That was the day his father had died.

He wished he could have told his father about the golden bird. But he couldn't tell his mother. She was too busy, too tired, too sad.

On the morning of the play, Andrew's mother went down to the school. She waited for Mr Swain to park his motorbike and take off his crash helmet, and then she went up to him. She could see Andrew sitting all by himself in the yard, while a group of children swept past him. Suddenly he spread his arms out and wheeled round, then just as suddenly he stood still again, as if he knew he was being watched.

'Could I have a word with you, Mr Swain? I'm worried about Andrew,' she said. 'Just look at him! He's doing that kind of thing all the time at home, pecking and bobbing his head, moving his arms up and down every time he thinks I'm not watching. Do you know – he seems to think he's a bird!'

To her surprise, Mr Swain only laughed. 'It's all right,' he told her. 'He's only practising for the school play. Didn't you know about it?'

Andrew's mother shook her head. 'He never tells me anything.'

'Come and see it tonight,' Mr Swain said. 'I

think you'll enjoy it!'

Andrew's mother looked across at her son as he bobbed his golden head from side to side. 'I think I will,' she said.

That afternoon the final rehearsal was held. For the very first time the children rehearsed in their costumes. Everything went wrong. The jugglers dropped their juggling balls, the fairies got the giggles, the king forgot two of his speeches, Sleeping Beauty had hiccoughs when she was supposed to be in a deep sleep. And when Andrew's moment came to stand behind her and spread out his wings as if he was going to fly off in search of the prince, he found he couldn't move. He couldn't lift his arms up, or turn his head, or bend his knees, or anything. He was frozen with fright.

'What use is that golden bird?' said Lynne as they were all hanging up their costumes. 'He might just as well be a stick insect!'

Chapter Five

AT SEVEN O'CLOCK the children could hear the buzz of the audience as the school hall began to fill up. They stood, nervous and excited, behind the curtain, waiting for the moment when Mr Swain would lift his hand and the musicians would start to play. They were all anxious because of the mistakes they had made at the dress rehearsal, but Mr Swain promised them that everything would be all right.

'You'll be wonderful,' he said. 'Enjoy it!' He lifted up his hand, and they were on!

Andrew had to wait a long time before his turn came to go on stage. He felt his stomach growing cold inside him. He felt sick and trembling. The music and the laughter, the singing and the applause, swirled round him in waves. He wanted to go home. He wanted to crawl into the quiet darkness of his bed and never come out again.

Then at last he felt Mr Swain's hand on his shoulder.

'Now, Andrew!'

He heard the children singing on stage,

'Golden bird, keep her safe,
Golden bird, keep her safe,
Guard her from all harm.'

He stepped onto the stage. The lights dazzled him. He paused for a moment, then tried to remember exactly what he had seen when he had watched the birds playing in the yard.

He bent his knees a little, so his back could curve over. He stretched out his neck. He peered straight down his nose, and cocked his head in little jerks and bobs from side to side. He forgot everything except the little bird-like movements he was making.

Now he could feel a hush descending on the room. The Sleeping Beauty and the king and queen and all the courtiers were asleep, and only he could save them. He flexed his

shoulder blades. That was where his wings
started from. He bent his elbows into his sides
then slowly, slowly, lifted them up and
stretched out his arms as far as they would
go. There was a gasp from the audience. His
golden feathers fluttered up around him as he
lifted his wings above his head. He rose on
his feet and crouched down again, rose again,
then stroked the air with his wings.

Again and again he lifted himself up, and at

last he felt the air turn below him. He tucked
his legs in and away out again as if he was
swimming, and he thrust his wings slowly
down and up, down and up. Far below him
he could see the people of the audience, their
faces upturned and their mouths round holes
of astonishment and joy. He could feel the air
rushing past him like water, he could hear it
whispering through his feathers. He could see
around him all the lights of the stars in the
night sky, and his wings
gleamed gold in the
moonlight.

Chapter Six

'YOU WERE BRILLIANT!' Lynne shouted. 'I don't know how you did that! You were brilliant!'

Andrew gazed round him. He was standing in the middle of the stage, and the audience were cheering and clapping and shouting. He had to go forward again and again to bow to them.

And when the curtain came down at last the king and queen and Sleeping Beauty and the prince and the cook and all the fairies were patting his shoulders and congratulating him. Mr Swain was beaming at him.

And then he saw his mother. She was full of smiles, just as she used to be. She knelt down and hugged him.

'I wish your dad could have seen you!' she said.

'So do I,' said Andrew. 'But I'm glad you came, Mum.'

He looked round at Mr Swain, and at all the smiling friends, and he knew that he was happy again.

Yellow Bananas are bright, funny, brilliantly imaginative stories written by some of today's top writers. All the books are beautifully illustrated in full colour.

So if you've enjoyed this story, why not pick another one from the bunch?

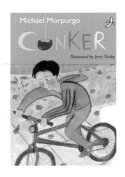